MASTER OF THE BEASTS

SHAMANI
THE RAGING
FLAME

With special thanks to Allan Frewin Jones

To Bodhi Churchill

www.beastquest.co.uk

ORCHARD BOOKS
338 Euston Road, London NW1 3BH
Orchard Books Australia
Level 17/207 Kent St, Sydney, NSW 2000

A Paperback Original
First published in Great Britain in 2012

Beast Quest is a registered trademark of Beast Quest Limited
Series created by Beast Quest Limited, London

Text © Beast Quest Limited 2012
Inside illustrations by Pulsar Estudio (Beehive Illustration)
Cover by Steve Sims © Beast Quest Limited 2012

A CIP catalogue record for this book is available from
the British Library.

ISBN 978 1 40831 519 4

3 5 7 9 10 8 6 4

Printed and bound by CPI Group (UK) Ltd, Croydon, CR0 4YY

The paper and board used in this paperback are natural recyclable
products made from wood grown in sustainable forests. The
manufacturing processes conform to the environmental regulations of
the country of origin.

Orchard Books is a division of Hachette Children's Books,
an Hachette UK company

www.hachette.co.uk

SHAMAN
THE RAGING
FLAME

BY ADAM BLADE

ORCHARD

So... You still wish to follow Tom on his Beast Quest.

Turn back now. A great evil lurks beneath Avantia's earth, waiting to arise and conquer the kingdom with violence and rage. Six Beasts with the hearts of Ancient Warriors, at the mercy of the Evil Wizard, Malvel, who I fear has reached the height of his powers.

War awaits us all.

I beg you, again, close this book and turn away. Evil will rise. Darkness will fall.

Your friend,
Wizard Aduro

PROLOGUE

Baburchi steadied himself as the mountain path crumbled under his foot. Earth and stones plunged into the deep valley. He leant against the cliff face that stretched away behind him, listening as the echoes of the falling rocks faded.

A slow grin spread over the hunter's weather-beaten face.

"You won't catch me out like that, old mountain," he growled. "It'll take more than a few loose pebbles to shake me from your side!"

He peered over the edge of the path. The mountain dropped away in folds and creases to the distant lowlands, where white rivers rushed and pine forests blanketed the foothills. An eagle soared below him through the air, half way between him and the valley floor.

Baburchi liked it way up here where only the goats dared to tread. He preferred to be as far as possible from the village people, with their foolish rules and regulations.

And he had good reason to be where the air was thin and clear. He was following paw-prints. He had first spotted the tracks much lower down on the narrow winding path.

"The tracks of a big wild cat, or I'm no hunter!" he'd said to himself. "I've never seen such huge prints. Three times the width of my hand! The pelt of such an animal will be worth a fortune!"

And so he had climbed, his crossbow bouncing on his back as he tracked the prints towards the high, snow-filled passes. He often had to use both his hands as he made his way nimbly up the precarious track.

"It will be worth it," he muttered to himself. "I'll be the richest man in the village!"

A sound from just ahead brought him to a halt. The path curved sharply around a shoulder of rock. Baburchi's hunter's senses tingled. Was he closing in on the animal? He slid his crossbow from his back and silently fitted a bolt to the string.

Soft-footed, he rounded the bend.

The goat path zigzagged steeply up the mountain, clinging to the rock-edge and lined with massive boulders.

"Where are you, my beauty?" Baburchi breathed.

A tall shape appeared from behind a boulder. Baburchi's finger twitched and the crossbow bolt hissed through the air.

"No!" he cried. It wasn't the cat – it was a man – a knight clad head to foot in black armour.

The bolt sparked as it glanced off the knight's breastplate.

The huge silent man blocked the path ahead. A visor hid his face.

His gloved hands gripped a wooden flail.

Baburchi eyed the figure nervously, licking his lips. He stared at the knight's armoured boots. Why had he not left any tracks? Those boots should have left deep impressions in the soil.

"I'm sorry," Baburchi said. "I didn't realise..."

There was something uncanny about the knight's armour – it glistened in the sunlight as though

its surface was slithering with oil. And why was he carrying such a strange weapon?

"Who are you?" Baburchi asked. "What are you doing so high on the mountain?"

A low rasping laugh came from the darkness behind the visor. His eyes glistened like burning coals.

Baburchi wasn't easily frightened, but there was something inhuman about the Black Knight – something fiendish. He began to back away, all thoughts of the big cat forgotten in his desire to be off the mountain.

The knight swung his flail in dizzying arcs.

Baburchi turned and fled, bounding down the mountain path. He dared not take his eyes off the uneven ground as he ran, but he could hear the thud of armoured feet pursuing him. The long shadow of the knight – thrown against the rock – kept pace.

Baburchi stumbled around a bend, sweat breaking out over his forehead. His heart crashed against his ribs and his lungs ached for more air. But as he ran, he saw the shape of the knight's shadow begin to change.

He's transforming into some other form! Baburchi thought in terror.

Whimpering with dread, Baburchi felt the ground slide away under his feet. He fell headlong, sprawling on the ground. The shadow loomed. Baburchi twisted onto his back and stared in horror at the creature that stood over him.

The knight was gone. In his place stood a giant black cheetah. Its eyes burned like furnaces, its body was solid and compact, seething with powerful muscles. Where the helmeted head had been, Baburchi saw black lips drawn back to reveal long white fangs against the red of a gaping throat.

With a huge roar that shook the mountain, the cheetah leapt forwards.

CHAPTER ONE

BEAST IN PERIL

"Come on, Storm," Tom said. "We're almost out of this horrible place!"

Tom led his brave stallion on through the smouldering remains of the great forest. Elenna and Silver were close by, the wolf leaping the blackened trunks of fallen trees while Elenna clambered over the dreadful wreckage of the fire.

Heavy clouds of smoke hung low in

the sky. Here and there a few trees still burned fitfully and scraps of hot ash danced in the air.

Tom used his sword to hack down the charred branches that blocked their path. In his mind he could still see Noctila the Death Owl swooping, the Evil Beast's cruel talons outstretched, his wings shedding burning tar that had set the forest ablaze.

It had been a fearsome battle. Even with the help of Tagus the Horse-Man, they had only just managed to gain victory over the rampaging creature.

Once the Death Owl had been defeated, he had shrunk and changed back into the shape of a knight with silver armour. And at that moment, the knight had vanished, returning to his long sleep in the Gallery of Tombs.

A sack hung from Storm's saddle,

containing magical objects given to them by the Good Wizard Aduro when he had sent them on this Quest. Tom frowned as he remembered his last glimpse of their old friend, his eyes red-rimmed, and his face grey with anxiety.

"This will be your most challenging Quest," he had told them. "Eternal darkness may fall over the kingdom of Avantia if you fail. I sense the coming of powerful evil!"

Aduro had taken them to the Gallery of Tombs – a chamber that lay beneath the castle of King Hugo. Here, they had discovered that the six Knights of Forton – protectors of old Avantia – had been awakened from their tombs. An ancient prophecy told that one day, when Avantia was in direst need, the six knights would rise from their slumber and battle to save the kingdom.

But Malvel had twisted the prophecy to his own wicked ends – awakening the knights and filling them with the spirits of Evil Beasts. Where once they had been a force for good, now they sought to destroy the six Good Beasts of Avantia that Tom and Elenna had saved in their first ever Quest.

Tom led Storm onwards, knowing that there were still five of the corrupted knights loose. He had to find and defeat them all.

"I see the edge of the forest!" Tom called to Elenna. Beyond the last few blackened trees, lay a landscape of wide, rolling hills.

They emerged into bright sunlight. Tom looked at Elenna. "You're covered in soot!" he said.

"So are you," Elenna retorted, wiping her sleeve across her face. "So are all four of us." Silver and Storm were also dirty from the fire.

"I see a stream!" said Elenna, pointing to where a ribbon of white water bubbled in a nearby dip in the land. "We can wash there."

They went to the stream and quickly washed off the worst of the black smears.

As the sun dried his face, Tom took out the marble globe that Aduro had given him. He gazed into its polished surface, hoping to see the path that they needed to follow.

The globe rose from his cupped hands and hovered in the air in front of them, spinning slowly and shedding light.

The globe came to a halt and settled down into Tom's palms. They could see the blackened forest illuminated on the

surface – and threading out from the
darkness, a slender line – a path that
led over the hills and away towards the
Northern Mountains.

"That's Colton," Elenna said,
pointing to a small town that lay in the
foothills of the mountains, close to the
snaking pathway.

Tom remembered the town from their
first adventure in those high mountains.

"I think I can guess the next Good Beast Malvel wishes to kill!" he said. He slid his shield off his back. "There! Look!" he cried. Sure enough, the feather given to them by Arcta the Mountain Giant was fading and wilting, as though it was about to crumble to nothingness.

"Arcta needs us!" Tom said, putting the globe away and leaping into the saddle. "Come on! We've no time to lose!"

Elenna jumped up behind him and in a few moments Storm was galloping full tilt towards the mountains, with Silver loping along at his side.

Tom set his jaw, his eyes already straining for a sight of their next enemy.

But which knight will Malvel use to attack us? thought Tom. *And how hard will it be to defeat him in battle?*

Only time and courage would tell.

CHAPTER TWO

THE CRUEL WHIP

As they galloped across the hills, the peaks of the mountains reared closer against the blue sky. From a distance, the Northern Mountains looked beautiful and serene, but Tom knew all too well how dangerous and inhospitable those snowy peaks could be for anyone who ventured into them.

"We haven't come by this route

before," Elenna said as they sped over the long grass. A broad, swift river ran through a valley just ahead of them. Willow trees dipped their hanging branches in the rushing water and the banks were lined with tall reeds.

"Our road runs alongside the river for a while," said Tom.

"At least we won't go thirsty," said Elenna. "But I wish there were some fruit trees nearby. I'm so hungry. Can you hear my stomach growling?"

Tom looked over his shoulder and grinned at her. "I can!" he said. "But I was too polite to mention it."

Elenna smiled and glanced at Silver. He was running alongside them with his tongue lolling. "We could all do with some food and water inside us," Elenna said.

Tom saw a wide track of beaten

earth winding down the side of the valley towards them. "I think we may be in luck. There's a road," said Tom. "People must live close by. And where there are people there will be food."

The river curved around a bend in the valley. A town came into view. The wooden buildings were newly thatched or roofed with bright red tiles. A stone bridge spanned the river and there was a large water mill at the river's edge, its great wooden wheel unmoving as the water churned past.

"We've nothing to exchange for food," said Tom. "Let's hope the people are hospitable to hungry travellers."

They trotted along the road into the town. A few people paused to watch them as they rode by and some frowned and backed away at the sight of Silver.

"Don't worry," Elenna called. "He's quite friendly."

As they reached the heart of the town, they heard a man's agonized screams. "That doesn't sound so friendly." Tom said grimly. "Someone's being hurt!"

He flicked the reins, urging Storm into a canter.

They came to a wide square where many people were gathered. The villagers had formed a ring, and in the centre was a man on his knees, his shirt torn away and his bent back raw from a flogging. A huge man stood over him, clad in a leather jerkin. His muscles bulged as he raised his arm and a vicious looking whip uncoiled for another blow.

"Hey!" Tom shouted. "Stop that!"

He jumped down from Storm's
back and pushed his way through
the crowd.

The whip came down again and
the cowering man's anguished cries
echoed across the square.

"I said stop that!" demanded Tom,
drawing his sword.

The whip was raised yet again, but Elenna pulled an arrow from her quiver and shot from her vantage point on Storm's back. The arrow ran swift and true, slicing through the leather whip.

The remnants of the whip snapped back, curling around the man's wrist. He cried out in pain. He turned, his eyes ferocious as he stared at Elenna.

"You dare to attack me?" he snarled, lumbering forwards. "You'll pay for that!"

"No she won't, you brute!" cried Tom, lifting his sword. "Keep back!"

The man's eyes burned with fury as Tom marched across the square and stood in front of him. "I am a friend to King Hugo and the Good Wizard Aduro," he said. "There are people at the Palace who will be interested to

hear of the brutality taking place
in this town."

The man's eyes narrowed and his
face grew pale. "That may be," he said
warily. "But the punishment to the
man was deserved."

"I doubt any crime deserves such
a whipping," Tom retorted.

He heard the voices of the
townsfolk rising around him.

"He deserved every blow!"
someone shouted.

"Each drop of blood was well spilt!"
called another.

Tom looked at the angry crowd.
"Was there a fair trial?" he called.
Tom saw Elenna jump down from
Storm's back and hurry over to kneel
beside the whipped man. He was
curled up on the ground, his knees up
to his chest and his arms shielding his

face as the breath came rasping from his throat.

"Even if you do think it was fair, it's over now," Elenna said. "He's suffered enough."

But the crowd began to move threateningly forwards. The big man gave Tom a spiteful look.

"Now you will learn the punishment given to strangers who interfere in our town!" he said.

Tom gripped his sword as he watched the approaching villagers. The last thing he wanted to do was fight, but one or two of them were clutching clubs, and there were others with long scythes. They closed in.

In his desire to help the whipped man, Tom realised he'd put himself and his friends in terrible danger.

CHAPTER THREE

BROKEN WHEEL

"Stop this, my good people!" called
a voice. An old man in smart clothes
stepped from the crowd. "We want
no ill-feeling between the town and
friends of the King."

Tom eyed him warily as the
advancing villagers came to a halt.

The new figure turned to Tom
and Elenna with a smile on his face.
"Come now, let hot tempers cool off,"

he said. "Yarl, you've proved your point."

The thickset man with the whip backed off.

This old man must be a respected member of the community, Tom thought.

"Strangers should not be so quick to judge," Yarl said. "You do not have all the facts! Egor here wrecked the wheel on my mill."

"How do you know he did it?" asked Tom, sheathing his sword and gesturing to the injured Egor. "Was he seen?"

Yarl grumbled, but the old man nodded towards an inn that stood to one side of the town square. "Come and take food and drink with us," he said.

"And you shall learn what happened," Yarl added.

"That's very kind of you. We would be honoured," Tom replied, but he gave Elenna a look that suggested they should both stay on their guard.

Elenna slipped her bow over her shoulder and turned to her wolf. "Silver," she said. "You and Storm must stand guard over this man while we are away. Don't let anyone near him."

While the two loyal animals moved close to the victim, Tom and Elenna followed Yarl and the older man across the square. They entered a long low-ceilinged room, thick with the sweet-smelling smoke from an open log fire. Rough tables and benches filled the floor and the walls were yellow with age.

"Landlord!" called Yarl. "Food and drink for our guests!"

Tom and Elenna were shown to a table. Yarl and the old man sat with them while others watched with cautious interest.

Soon Tom and Elenna had plates of meat and steaming vegetables in front of them. "Thank you," said Tom as they began to eat. "We're both very hungry."

"You are most welcome," said the old man. "My name is Aaron, and I'm the mayor of this town."

Tom looked at him. "Our animals are also in need of food and water, if that isn't too much trouble."

The old man nodded. "Of course, I shall see to it."

As the two friends ate hungrily, Aaron leaned back, his thumbs in his belt. "This is a quiet town," said the old man, "and we seldom have the

opportunity to welcome important folk from outside. But a few days ago, we were honoured by a visit from a knight clad from head to foot in the finest black armour I have ever seen."

Tom stared at the man, his fork half way to his mouth. The hairs on the back of his neck prickled at the mention of the knight. He glanced

quickly at Elenna, shaking his head
a little to let her know not to say
anything. He wanted to know more
before they spoke.

"Our welcoming doors were thrown
open to our distinguished guest,"
Aaron continued. "We organized
a mighty feast to which every man,
woman and child was invited."

"We let our guard down," added
Yarl. "More fool us!"

"What happened?" asked Tom.

"After we feasted, everyone fell
asleep. Egor slipped into the town and
damaged my mill wheel," said Yarl.
"He owns a mill a few miles further
down the river and he has long envied
the fact that I am more prosperous
than him." Yarl hammered his fist on
the table. "He is a sly and a devious
man, and he deserved every stripe

I gave him with my whip." He looked sharply at Tom. "Now do you see why he had to be punished?"

"May I see the mill wheel?" Tom asked.

"What business is it of yours?" roared Yarl.

Beyond the man's back, Tom could see the town square through the window of the inn. The whipped man sat between Storm and Silver.

"Tend to the man's wounds and I'll help you," Tom said.

"How can you help us, boy?" asked Yarl.

"If you show me the damage done to the wheel, I will send word back to the Palace," Tom explained. "I'll ask King Hugo to send his best carpenters to repair it." He looked steadily at Yarl. "But I'll do nothing for you unless that man's wounds are tended to."

Yarl nodded. "Very well," he said. "Egor shall receive medicine." He stood up. "Come with me and see what damage he did in his envy and spite!"

Tom and Elenna followed Yarl and Aaron through a back entrance from the inn. From there it was only a short walk to the sturdy timber-built mill.

They came to the riverbank. Spray filled the air where the rushing river struck against the immobile wheel. Tom could see broken shards of wood jutting out where the spokes had been smashed.

Something caught his eye, glinting in the sunlight, high on the back of the wheel. Tom moved closer and climbed cautiously up the wheel. It shuddered under him and the rumble of the river filled his ears. Adjusting his balance and holding on firmly, he reached up and closed his fingers around the shining thing.

He prised it loose from the wood.

The object was triangular and curved and wider than his hand. Tom shivered with dread as he stared at the thing.

It was a razor-sharp amber claw.

CHAPTER FOUR

DEADLY FOE

"What are you doing up there?" called Yarl.

Tom glanced down over his shoulder. "I thought I saw something," he said, slipping the amber claw into his tunic. He didn't think it was wise to talk of Evil Beasts in front of the townsfolk. He climbed down.

"So you've seen the damage Egor did!" said Yarl.

"I see that it has been damaged,"

Tom replied. "But there is no proof that Egor was responsible."

With a snort, Yarl turned away and joined a group of townsfolk.

Tom moved close to Elenna and briefly gave her a glimpse of the claw. "A Beast has done this," he whispered.

"They won't believe that," said Elenna. "They'll carry on whipping Egor."

"Not while there's blood in my veins, they won't," Tom responded. "We'll get him away from… Ahhh!" A pain like a thunderbolt struck him between the temples. He staggered, clutching his head, seeing flashes of white fire in front of his eyes.

"Tom, what is it?" gasped Elenna, reaching out to steady him.

"I hear…a voice…" groaned Tom. "Crying out…roaring in pain…" The agony in his head softened and he stared at Elenna. "It's Arcta – something's wrong! We have to get to him now." He glanced towards the group of townspeople. "We mustn't let them know what's going on." He steadied himself, refusing to give in to the pain. He looked into Elenna's concerned eyes. "We'll take Egor with us."

The two friends moved away from the mill, making for the town square.

"Hey!" called one of the people. "How quickly can you get word to King Hugo and have him send carpenters to us?"

"We'll do what we can," Tom said.

"And what do you mean by that?" demanded Yarl, blocking their way. "Are you the King's friend or not?"

Tom's lips tightened and he rested his hand on the hilt of his sword.

"Silver!" shouted Elenna. "To me!"

Her loyal wolf came bounding towards them, growling and baring his teeth. The townsfolk backed away and Tom and Elenna ran for the square.

"Stop them!" shouted Yarl. "They've lied to us!"

Aaron called for calm, but his voice was drowned out.

Tom drew his sword and Elenna notched an arrow to the bowstring as they ran into the square, Silver racing at their side. The townspeople stared and shouted, but they dared not attack.

Storm was in the middle of the square, standing over the injured man. Tom sprang into the saddle. "Lift him up to me," he called to Elenna. Using all her strength, Elenna helped the injured man to his feet.

"They're taking Egor!" someone shouted. "Stop them!" A stone flung by one of the townsfolk sped past Tom's head.

They aren't going to let us leave, Tom thought.

Tom grasped the man's belt and heaved him up across Storm's back. A moment later, Elenna was seated behind him. With a flick of the reins, Tom sent Storm cantering across the square. Townspeople dived aside as they raced past.

As they left town, the angry voices died away.

"Where the road divides, follow the river path," Egor gasped weakly. "My homestead is not far from here." He breathed heavily. "Be sure to keep to the dirt track because there are treacherous quicksands by the river. We'd be swallowed up, horse and all, if we strayed into one."

They came to a cluster of wooden buildings with a paddock and a small mill. A black and white dog came running out, barking in greeting. Egor climbed down awkwardly from Storm's back.

"Faithful Shep!" he gasped as the dog raced towards him. "All's well, I'm back!"

But the words had hardly left his lips when something huge and fast-moving came hurtling across their path. Tom recognized the creature as it leapt on the dog, its teeth snapping and its vicious tusks stabbing.

"Watch out!" Tom cried. "It's a Varkule!"

Tom knew these foul-smelling monsters all too well. Each of the knights had one of these hyena-like creatures as a 'pet' – its appearance must mean that their enemy was close by.

Silver gave a howl and sprang forwards as the Varkule and the helpless sheepdog rolled over and over in the dirt.

"Silver, you'll be killed!" cried Elenna.

The fearless wolf leapt at the writhing animals, and Tom realized that he was too far away to help.

CHAPTER FIVE

TRAPPED!

The noble wolf landed on the
Varkule's back, sinking his fangs into
the monster's thick hide. The Varkule
reared up in pain, twisting its neck
to try and gore Silver with its tusks.
It roared and snorted, the strip of fur
along its spine prickling up, as stiff
as wire.

Tom raced after them, gagging from
the stench of the hideous creature.

"Silver! Be careful!" cried Elenna, running alongside, an arrow to her bow but unable to get a clear target as the wolf and the Varkule fought and struggled. The Varkule's feet stamped loudly as it staggered across the ground.

Silver sprang free, howling in anger.

The Varkule got to its feet, but even as it lowered its ugly head, its tusks thrusting forwards, the wolf jumped high and came down with his mouth wide.

The Varkule's neck arched upwards as Silver bit deep into the flesh of its shoulder. It let out a howl of anguish as Silver sprang back, his jaws dripping blood.

"Well done, Silver!" shouted Tom, running at the Varkule with his sword raised.

The giant hyena turned away and went lumbering off, limping heavily as the blood gushed from its wound.

Tom chased after it with grim determination.

If I can keep it in sight, it will lead me to its master! Tom thought.

As he ran, he heard Egor's

voice calling: "Beware!"

He raced on. The Varkule was only a few paces in front of him now, grunting and spilling blood. He heard Elenna panting as she caught up with him.

Suddenly the Varkule came to a stumbling halt. Howling and straining, the monster struggled desperately as its feet sank into the soft boggy ground.

A moment later, Tom was aware of the ground giving way under his own feet. He floundered, sinking to his ankles in green ooze, trying to turn and pull himself free of the quagmire. He stared downwards – the slime was rising up around his shins.

"The quicksands!" he gasped. "Elenna – get back!" This was what Egor had been warning them about.

Tom threw himself backwards, pulling one foot out of the sucking slime. He felt firm ground under his foot. Pushing down hard, he ripped his other leg from the mire and staggered back the way they had come, pulling Elenna with him.

They watched as the thrashing Varkule sank deeper. It tossed its head to and fro, its mouth wide as it howled in terror, eyes rolling white with panic.

Elenna looked away as the monster finally disappeared into the quicksand. A few thick bubbles rose to the surface, then the slimy earth closed over the doomed creature.

"What was that thing?"

Tom turned at the sound of Egor's voice. He was trudging up behind them, Shep close to his legs and whimpering in fear. "What is happening in Avantia?"

Tom shuddered, overwhelmed by the danger that was spreading like an evil plague through the kingdom.

"These are bad times," he told Egor. "Stay safe behind bolted doors – we will do what we can."

They made their way back to Egor's homestead. "You did well!" Elenna told Silver, stroking his fur.

They mounted Storm and after

a brief farewell, they rode off.

Tom looked towards the mountains. "The knight must have left the Varkule here to slow us down," he said grimly. "But nothing is going to stop us from fulfilling our Quest."

They left the river behind and made their way into a landscape of buckled foothills. The mountains rose ahead against the sky, white as fangs, sharp and dangerous. As determined as he was, Tom felt the weight of the Quest bearing down on him. Sometimes it seemed as though his duty to protect Avantia would never end.

He glanced up as the air shimmered. Puzzled, he reined Storm in, running his hands over his eyes.

"All of Avantia is relying on you," whispered a familiar voice from out of nowhere.

The air swirled in front of them
and suddenly Aduro was there, a
reassuring vision hanging a finger's
breadth above the ground.

The Good Wizard's hand reached
towards them, his eyes haunted. "See
what will happen if you do not reach
the mountains in time!" he declared.

As he spoke a bruise of darkness
opened up in the air between them.

Tom and Elenna saw Arcta and a knight in black armour battling on a mountain peak. Even as they watched, Arcta cried out in anguish and fell under the relentless blows of the Black Knight's weapon – it looked like a flail used to thresh corn. "Behold he who will become Shamani, the Raging Flame!" cried the Wizard.

"No!" Tom cried, but the vision had already faded away.

"Be swift!" came Aduro's voice from the air. "Or all will be lost!"

Tom snatched out the globe map, seeing the path heading northwards. "We daren't stop!" he said. "We'll ride through the night!" He pressed his heels into Storm's sides, urging him into a gallop, Silver streaking along at their side.

Night fell as they forged on. The stars

glittered like flecks of ice in the black sky and the cold air came sweeping down out of the mountains. Silver's fur flashed a ghostly grey in the gloom, and the white steam rose in plumes from Storm's nostrils.

Higher and higher they climbed through the mountains, desperate for some sign of their friend, the Good Beast Arcta.

They were still heading upwards, when the first light of dawn shone in the sky. Tom scoured the tumbled mountains with tired eyes. Where was the Black Knight? Were they too late?

A loud groan echoed from the peaks. Tom brought Storm to a halt. "What was that?" he asked, listening intently.

"Arcta!" cried Elenna. "He's in pain!"

Another groan sounded. Tom rose in his stirrups, staring around them, trying to pinpoint the direction from which the sounds were coming.

A third groan shivered in the air.

"That way!" Tom cried, flicking the reins so that Storm turned and trotted towards a high wall of rock.

"I don't see him," Elenna gasped. "Where is he?"

Tom stared around himself in confusion, a patch of rocks ahead tumbled loose. From a crevice between two boulders, a great hairy hand reached out, pawing the ground near Tom's leg.

"It's Arcta," Tom cried. "We've found him at last, but he's trapped!"

CHAPTER SIX

CLAWS OF AMBER

As Tom reached down to grasp Arcta's outstretched hand, the great fingers slid away between the boulders.

"Arcta!" Tom shouted, throwing himself from the saddle and peering into the inky blackness between the rocks. "Don't despair!" he called into the gloom. "We're here to help."

"How did he become trapped like that?" asked Elenna, jumping down at Tom's side.

"I don't know," Tom replied, stretching his arms around one of the boulders. "Help me try to move this!" Elenna put her back to the rock and heaved with all her might. There was a creak and a rumble.

"It's working!" gasped Tom. "A little more effort!" The sweat prickled on his brow as he used every muscle and sinew in his body to strain against the heavy boulder.

They gave a cry of triumph as the rock shifted sideways with a grinding rumble, revealing a deep black crack.

"There are caves in there!" said Elenna.

Tom turned and patted Storm's neck. "We won't be away long," he reassured the horse. "You stay here with Silver."

"Silver, no!" shouted Elenna – but she was too late, the wolf had already sprung through the crack.

"Quickly," said Tom. "Follow him."

"We'll need a light," said Elenna. She upended her quiver and a small flint fell out. She tugged up some dry grass and twisted it together. Striking the flint against a stone, she ignited the slender taper. "It won't last long," she warned.

Tom nodded. "We'll have to move quickly," he said.

Elenna slipped through the gap with Tom close behind. The flame revealed a cave with a high roof. It was cold and clammy inside and the cracked walls ran with moisture. A wide tunnel led into deeper blackness.

Tom heard heavy footfalls lumbering away down the winding tunnel.

It must be Arcta – but why was he running away from them?

"Arcta! Come back!" Tom shouted. Drawing his sword and gripping his shield tightly, Tom ran along at Elenna's side into the belly of the mountain.

Tom could no longer hear the Mountain Giant's running feet, but their own footsteps echoed ominously, and shadows crept and slunk along behind them. The crooked tunnel showed signs of having been worked at – there were deep gouges and cuts in the walls, and shards of stone were scattered across the uneven floor. They saw broken chisels and mallets on the ground and every so often they passed abandoned wooden carts with iron wheels.

"I think this was a mine," said Tom.

They emerged into a cavern where battered weapons and armour lay rusting on the floor. The light glinted on a dented helmet. Pieces of a broken sword lay on the ground. An old breastplate gleamed in the flame. "An armoury, perhaps?" suggested Elenna.

"I've never heard of a place like this," Tom said. He halted and held up his hand. "Listen!"

Roars came booming down the tunnel. "Arcta!" Tom said. He raced onwards into the darkness.

He heard Elenna's feet pattering along close behind. Already he could see daylight up ahead.

"Tom, be careful!" Elenna shouted.

Tom emerged into the open under a wide blue sky. He realised he had come right through the mountain. He was on a slim ledge of stone above a giddying fall. The mountainside sloped steeply away below him. A narrow path with rusted metal tracks along it zigzagged down the mountainside to a terrible sight: Arcta and the Black Knight were further down the path, doing battle on the brink of a sheer drop.

Now Tom understood why the Mountain Giant had been running

– he must have been pursuing the knight through the tunnels.

Arcta loomed over the knight, his long arms reaching out to grasp his enemy, his fangs bared. But the Black Knight was armed with his own deadly weapon. Tom saw that it was sturdier than a farmer's flail – two batons of gnarled wood joined by a short chain. The air shrieked as the knight swung the terrible weapon around his head.

As Tom watched, the knight lurched to one side, hitting the back of Arcta's legs with the flail. The Beast howled in pain, stumbling and losing his balance.

For a moment, Tom feared that Arcta might topple off the path, but the Beast clung to the rock and steadied himself, snarling in anger.

The knight moved back, but even

as he did so, Tom and Elenna saw his shape begin to change. Roaring, the Knight's form distorted and melted – he was becoming a Beast!

"Shamani, the Raging Flame!" muttered Tom, remembering Aduro's warning.

In less than three beats of Tom's heart, the knight was gone and a gigantic black cheetah stood in his place. It raked the ground with glowing orange claws, sending up shards of stone and sparks.

"The amber claw!" gasped Tom. Now he knew how the mill wheel had been damaged. "The evil Beast must have attacked the town!" he cried. "Not the Varkule!"

"We have to help Arcta," Elenna declared.

Tom nodded. *But how do we do that?*

he thought. Arcta and the Knight are too far away. "We won't be able to get to them in time," he exclaimed.

"We could use one of the old mining carts!" said Elenna, already running back into the tunnel.

Tom quickly saw what Elenna had in mind. The tracks that ran along the path had obviously been put there for the carts to run on – once one of those carts was on the steeply sloping path, it would go like the wind!

There was a cart close to the tunnel's end, and it took them only a few moments to drag it to the top of the path and heave it onto the tracks. Silver howled encouragement at their side.

They clung to the cart, looking at one another. "Ready?" asked Tom. Elenna nodded. They gave the cart a running start and as it gained momentum they leapt aboard. The cart rattled and clanked whilst gathering speed, juddering and shaking Tom's bones as it shot forwards.

Tom leant over the side, using his weight to keep the rattling cart on the narrow metal tracks.

The rusty wheels screamed in protest and the wind whistled in Tom's ears as the cart plunged down, trailing long ropes from where it had once been dragged through the mines. Tom hoped that Silver would be able to keep up.

They came to a tight bend in the path. Tom and Elenna hurled themselves to one side, using their combined weight to prevent the cart from coming off the tracks and plunging down the mountainside with them inside. They were closing in on Arcta and the Beast.

Sparks filled the air as Tom and
Elenna were thrown around another
sharp bend. But the cart's wheels
skidded on loose stones, shuddering
as it tipped over onto two wheels.

Tom clung grimly to the top of the
cart as the bone-crushing fall down
the mountain yawned beneath him.

CHAPTER SEVEN

CAT AND MOUSE

"Hold my legs!" Tom shouted to
Elenna as the cart teetered on the
very brink of the pathway. Elenna
launched herself forwards and
clung on grimly as Tom leant out,
just managing to snatch hold of the
withered branch of a gnarled old tree
that clung to the mountainside.

Tom gritted his teeth, his arms
almost pulled from their sockets as he

strained to keep a grip on the branch.

The cart crashed down on all four wheels again and they careered down the final long slope to where Arcta and Shamani faced one another. The Mountain Giant was bellowing and beating his fists against his chest while the gigantic cheetah hissed and tore at the air with his claws.

Shamani's black coat glistened with an oily sheen and his amber claws looked sharp enough to slice flesh from bones. He turned his furred head as the cart thundered down the tracks, his eyes burning with fierce red fire, his jaws flexing to reveal long dagger-like fangs.

Tom gripped his sword as he leant over the front of the cart. His hope was to strike first, but Shamani lurched back on his haunches and

swung his paw, hitting the cart and
bringing it to a halt that almost tipped
it off its wheels.

Elenna gave a cry of alarm as she
was thrown forward in the cart.
Behind them, Tom heard Silver
whining in fear. Tom clung on to
the rim of the cart with one hand,
his sword still ready in the other. He
shifted his weight to try and prevent

the cart from overbalancing, but still
it teetered on the brink of the long
fall as Shamani reared up in front of
them. One more blow and the cart
would be thrown off the pathway
with Tom and Elenna helpless inside.

Arcta's hands closed on Shamani's
whipping tail and the Evil Beast
twisted, snarling and clawing at the
Mountain Giant. The tail slipped from
Arcta's grip and he stumbled and fell
under Shamani's attack, his great
feet sliding from beneath him so that
he rolled over the edge of the path.
His long arms clung on grimly to the
edge, his body hanging above the
long drop.

Hissing, Shamani turned again to
stare with his furnace-red eyes at Tom
and Elenna. A huge claw sliced the
air. Tom ducked, only just managing

to avoid being cut to ribbons. He felt the cart rock again on the edge of the path. Above Shamani's enraged howling, Tom heard a familiar sound. It was a loud neighing. He lifted his head above the top of the cart and saw his brave stallion galloping at full speed up the pathway from below. Storm must have found a way around the mountain!

"Storm!" Tom cried. "Be careful!" He couldn't bear the thought of his friend being wounded by Shamani's claws.

The horse galloped on, jumping over Arcta's arms as the giant fought to pull himself up onto the path again. Shamani turned with a fearsome hiss, but Storm gave a mighty leap, sailing over the cheetah's back. As he came down onto the path again, he snatched at a trailing rope with his teeth, tugging at the tottering cart, pulling it back off the brink of the path so that it rolled rapidly away from the evil Beast.

"Well done, Storm!" shouted Tom.

Shamani's eyes flashed with fury at seeing his prey pulled to safety. Arcta clambered back onto the path behind the evil Beast.

Tom brandished his sword as he sprung from the cart and Elenna quickly fitted an arrow to her bow. Silver pounced down beside them.

Shamani spun this way and that, spitting foul saliva as he tried to choose his first victim. The Mountain Giant seemed about to throw himself at the Beast.

"No, Arcta!" Tom shouted.

The Good Beast stared at him for a moment, then roared and thumped his chest. Shamani twisted lithely and snatched at Arcta with a lethal paw. But Arcta did not fight back, instead he leapt onto the steep mountainside and began to swarm upwards, hand over hand, his great fingers and toes finding ledges and lips of rock as he climbed.

Arcta was making for the ledge

at the top of the pathway. Tom saw the Mountain Giant plunge into the tunnel, slamming his fists into the rock walls as he went.

Tom had no time to wonder at Arcta's strange behaviour. He braced himself for the cheetah's assault. "Elenna," he shouted, "I need a token from the saddlebag."

Aduro had given them six tokens to use against the six Beasts. He just hoped that Elenna chose wisely!

"I know which one," Elenna called back as she ran. "The piece of amber! It matches Shamani's claws!"

Shamani's foreleg raked at Tom. He ducked, swinging his sword and hearing it chime as it struck a claw and deflected the blow. Shamani hissed, swiping again. Tom leapt aside as the claws came raking down,

gouging the rocks.

The clawed paw fell a third time, and again Tom managed to dodge out of reach.

Tom smiled grimly to himself – this was like a deadly game of cat and mouse. *And if I am the mouse*, thought Tom, *then I'll make Shamani work hard for his prey!*

He leapt high over the Beast's back, coming down firmly on both feet behind the monster.

"I'm not so easily caught!" Tom declared as he slashed at the cheetah's tail, drawing blood.

Shamani howled, twisting quickly, his jaws wide as he pounced towards Tom. But Tom dived forwards, feeling the claws graze uncomfortably along his back as he rolled beneath Shamani's body.

As he found his feet and ran back up the path, he saw Elenna guiding Storm and Silver away so that they would not get caught up in the battle.

"Do you have the token?" Tom shouted to Elenna, his head spinning from all the ducking and diving.

Elenna held the lump of amber in her fist. Tom saw her eyes widen as he ran to take it from her. A moment later, a weight fell on his back. He felt claws raking, he heard the spitting of the evil Beast above him. He sprawled helplessly on the ledge as the great paw crushed him. He tasted blood on his lips.

The cat had caught the mouse!

CHAPTER EIGHT

THE BLACK KNIGHT

Tom could hardly move under the weight of Shamani's paw. Red spots of light flashed in front of his eyes as the air was crushed from his lungs. It felt like an iron band tightening around his chest.

The Evil Beast growled above him. Twisting his head, Tom saw the vile cheetah's gaping maw coming down

on him, teeth ready to tear into his flesh.

Using all that remained of his failing strength, Tom pulled his sword arm free. He swung his sword, the flat of the blade striking the Evil Beast on the nose. Shamani reared up, howling in agony.

The pressure on Tom lessened and he managed to squirm free. He was on his feet in an instant, but to his horror he realized that he had lost his shield. He saw it lying on the brink of the path.

He dived for it, but Shamani was quicker. The Beast came down between him and the shield, slashing at Tom with his claws. The monster's flicking tail caught the shield and sent it toppling over the edge of the path.

Tom gasped in dismay as his

precious shield plunged down the mountainside. How would he defend himself without it?

Shamani's eyes burned as he reared up and growled. Tom gripped his sword in both hands, waiting for the Beast to pounce.

An arrow sped through the air, but Shamani was too quick for Elenna's shafts. One paw lashed out, knocking it aside. A second arrow fared no better. And now there was a triumphant note in the Beast's roars – as though Shamani knew that nothing could stop him.

Tom braced himself for the Beast's next attack, but a roaring filled his ears from above. He glanced up. Arcta stood on the high ledge, clutching a huge boulder in both hands. With a bellow, the Mountain Giant hurled

the boulder down the mountainside
towards Shamani.

The Evil Beast swerved aside to
avoid the thundering missile.

"Thank you, Arcta!" Tom shouted.
Then he saw that the Good Beast
clutched a huge shield in his arms.

Arcta must have dragged it from the

armoury we saw in the tunnels,
Tom realized.

With another roar, Arcta flung the shield to Tom. It skidded down the mountain and Tom braced himself to catch it. It was massive – almost as tall as Tom himself! The weight threw Tom onto his back as he caught hold of it. He held it above him as Shamani pounced.

He winced as the Evil Beast's body smashed onto him. He heard the deadly claws gouging at the shield and smelled Shamani's foul breath all around him.

Tom knew he had to fight back or he would be squashed like a beetle. Pressing his shoulders to the shield, he flexed his legs, using all his strength to push against the Beast's weight.

Sweat poured down Tom's face as
he heaved upwards. If he failed, he
knew he would not have the strength
left for a second attempt. The Quest
would be over.

"I won't be beaten!" Tom shouted as

he lurched upright. He pushed harder against the growling Beast. Suddenly Shamani gave a howl of alarm.

He's on the edge of the path, Tom realised. *One more good push will send him over!*

Tom threw himself forwards behind the shield. With a howl of fear, Shamani plunged backwards over the ledge, his huge body writhing in the air as he fell.

Tom dropped to his knees, every muscle strained to its limit. He could hear branches cracking and breaking as the Beast tumbled down the mountain.

Nothing could survive such a fall.

"You did it!" gasped Elenna, running to Tom's side.

Tom staggered to his feet. "I never wanted to kill him," he panted. "The knights were made evil by Malvel's spell. It wasn't their fault."

He stumbled to the edge of the path, expecting to see the body of the Beast mangled on the rocks far below. But he lurched back in surprise – the monstrous cheetah was gone. Clinging grimly to the shreds of branches directly below him was the Black Knight.

The armoured warrior climbed steadily up towards them. Angry red eyes glared from the oily helmet. Wicked laughter filled the air.

"The amber token!" Tom urged, holding his hand out. "Quickly!"

Elenna dropped the lump of amber into Tom's hand. He glanced at it, wondering what its power might be. He stared in astonishment – frozen inside the amber was a perfectly preserved mosquito that he had not noticed before.

A black gauntlet snatched at Tom's leg. He gasped as he was tipped onto his back. The lump of amber fell from his hand, bouncing along the path before exploding into fragments.

"No!" Elenna shouted, as the knight's other hand caught her leg.

Tom kicked himself free of the Knight's grip and leapt to his feet, sword in hand and the heavy shield on his arm.

I've broken the token, he thought, close to despair. *I've failed!*

An angry buzzing sound above him made him turn and stare upwards. The mosquito from the amber crystal had come alive and was hovering in the air above his head.

"Tom, look!" cried Elenna, pointing

past the hovering insect.

At first Tom thought the darkness he saw pouring over the mountain peak was a strange storm cloud. But as it came rushing down through the air, it swirled and moved with a deadly purpose, growing larger and darker by the moment. And as it grew, a wild buzzing sound came with it.

"Mosquitoes!" Tom shouted in alarm above the rising noise of the vast swarm. "Thousands of them!"

CHAPTER NINE

THE HORROR FROM THE AIR

As the swarm swamped them, Tom swept his sword and shield this way and that, desperately trying to fend them off.

But he saw that it wasn't only mosquitoes that were attacking. There were black flying beetles, grasshoppers, dragonflies, locusts, blowflies...a whole host of different

insects. They flew into Tom's face,
snagging in his hair, landing on him
and crawling over his skin, seeking a
way under his clothes – blinding him,
filling his mouth and nostrils and
ears, their endless droning growing
like a roar inside his head.

The token must have summoned them, he realised.

He heard Elenna cry out, and saw her struggling in the dark swarm, her arms lashing, her whole body twisting this way and that as she tried vainly to get away from the dreadful creatures.

The insects gathered around Storm and Silver as well. The horse was panicking, rearing up, and neighing wildly, his hind hooves only inches from the lip of the path. Silver jumped to and fro, snapping and howling as the insects settled in his thick fur.

"Must get to the caves!" Tom shouted above the grating shriek of the insects. He stumbled desperately along the path, snatching at Storm's reins and pulling him along in his wake. Elenna and Silver ran after him through the clinging swarm.

As they came to the top of the path, the insects began to fall away. Tom slapped Storm's hindquarters, urging the animal into the tunnel. Elenna and Silver followed, but Tom hesitated a moment, his skin stinging from bites, his flesh crawling even though the insects were gone.

He leant over the ledge. Away down on the path, he saw a solid cloud of darkness. The insects were swarming around the Black Knight – flying so thickly that Tom could only see the knight's gauntleted hands and the top of his helmet as he writhed on the pathway. Tom heard him crying out as the insects flew in through his visor and through every crack and chink in his armour.

Elenna ran to Tom's side. "What's happening?" she asked, staring down.

"They're inside his armour!" Tom said.

Elenna threw her hands to her mouth. "Oh! How horrible!"

The Black Knight staggered along the pathway, thrashing wildly. He began to tear at his armour, ripping piece after piece from his body in his frantic desire to be rid of the insects. He tossed his helmet aside and his flail went clattering down the mountainside as he fell to his knees.

His breastplate clanged on the ground, he cast his gauntlets and greaves and chainmail vest aside until he was kneeling on the path in nothing but a leather jerkin and trousers.

Pity filled Tom. "I have to help him!" he said, already racing back down the long winding path. He heard Elenna's rapid footsteps following him. As he ran at full tilt down the pathway, Tom brandished his sword, shouting. "Get away!

Leave him alone!"

To his surprise, the dark clumps of insects that were infesting the knight's body took to the air as he approached and swarmed away down the mountain.

The knight was lying on the path now, his face ashen, his armour gone and his underclothes torn to shreds, his grey flesh pierced by a thousand red marks.

Tom fell to his knees at the knight's side.

"I won't let them come back," Tom told him. The man stared up at him, his eyes swimming, his lips white.

"It's as though they have drained all the blood from him," gasped Elenna, kneeling at Tom's side. She turned to Tom. "There's nothing I can do to help him!"

CHAPTER TEN

THE UNENDING QUEST

Tom pulled the man's head onto his lap, brushing the lank hair from his eyes. The knight was breathing in shallow gasps as he gazed up into Tom's face. "Once, long ago, I fought and defeated Shamani," he murmured from between his pale, drawn lips. "The cheetah was a fearsome Beast… It was a deadly battle…" He paused, gasping for breath, pain etched into every line of his face.

"I know," Tom said gently. "The Evil Wizard Malvel has cast a spell that turns the Knights of Forton into the Beasts they once defeated."

The knight grimaced in pain.

"Can we help him?" Elenna whispered.

The knight turned his head and gazed up at the sky. A strange light came into his eyes, as though he could see something floating above them.

He lifted himself a little, reaching up with one hand.

"Please keep still," Elenna urged him, her hand on his arm. She gave a gasp – as she touched the man's skin, he faded and her hand fell through him as though he were made of mist.

Then his body vanished completely.

"It's over," Tom said, wiping the back of his hand across his forehead. "Aduro must have transported him back to the Gallery of Tombs."

A roar from above made both of them look up. Arcta was standing on the high ledge, beating his chest with his great hands.

Tom picked up his sword and lifted it in a salute to the Good Beast. "All is well, Arcta!" he called. "The enemy is gone."

Arcta's mouth stretched into a smile – although he did not understand Tom's words, he clearly knew the meaning behind them. Waving one long hairy arm, Arcta turned away from the mountain ridge and shambled out of sight.

"He's going back to his mountaintop home," said Elenna.

Tom nodded. "And from there he'll keep a lookout over Avantia again." He sheathed his sword.

"You are correct," said a familiar voice. Tom turned in surprise. Aduro hung suspended in the air beyond the pathway. For a split second Tom was alarmed that the Good Wizard would fall – but then he realized that it was just a vision.

The wizard's voice was grave. "Your Quest has become even more urgent, my friends," Aduro told them, his eyes filled with anxiety. "Freya has sent me word that Malvel is planning a new way to get back into Avantia."

"He's trapped, isn't he?" said Tom.

The wizard frowned. "Your success in defeating the Knights of Forton has proved to him that his spell is not as powerful as he had hoped! He's angry."

"Can he get back to Avantia?" asked Elenna.

"We have to stay on our guard," growled the wizard. "Where Malvel's cunning is concerned, we can never be sure what may happen."

"And what will happen if he does manage to enter Avantia?" asked Tom.

But already the Good Wizard's image was fading.

"Be wary…be very wary…" whispered the voice. Then there was an eerie silence on the mountain as the Good Wizard vanished.

"We must go on," said Tom. He pointed down the long twisting path. "My shield is down there – we'll pick it up on the way." As he spoke, Storm and Silver came walking slowly down the path towards them.

Storm's ears were drawn back and his eyes were nervous – the stallion hadn't yet quite recovered from the insect attack. Silver pushed his muzzle into Elenna's hand, as though to let her know he was glad that they had all survived the ordeal.

They began the long descent from the mountain. Tom's flesh still stung from the bites of the insects and his muscles ached from his battle with Shamani. Every battle seemed to take more out of him.

How much longer can I go on like this? he wondered.

"Do you remember that flail the knight used in his battle with Arcta?" said Elenna. "It was a powerful weapon. I'd like to try and make something similar."

Tom nodded. "We will certainly need all the help we can get," he said. He was weary and bruised, and he knew that four more Knights of Forton awaited him on his Quest. Four more knights, warped by Malvel's evil – four more deadly Beasts to defeat.

"And Malvel himself could soon be in Avantia," he said. "That could turn out to be the most dangerous of all my Quests."

Elenna's hand came down on his shoulder. "Our Quests," she said with a brave smile. "You're not alone, Tom."

Tom returned her smile, new strength and purpose seeping into his tired body. "I know," he said, glancing from her to the two loyal animals. "And while there's blood in my veins

I'll never rest until Malvel is stopped forever!" He lifted his head, staring resolutely into the distance. "We've come too far to let him win!"

Join Tom on the next stage
of the Beast Quest when he meets

LUSTOR
THE ACID DART

DARE YOU DIVE IN?

Deep in the water lurks a new breed of Beast.

If you want the latest news and exclusive Sea Quest goodies, join our Sea Quest Club!

Visit www.seaquestbooks.co.uk/club and sign up today!

Join the Quest,
Join the Tribe

www.beastquest.co.uk

Have you checked out the Beast Quest website?
It's the place to go for games, downloads, activities,
sneak previews and lots of fun!

You can read all about your favourite Beasts, down-
load free screensavers and desktop wallpapers for
your computer, and even challenge your friends
to a Beast Tournament.

Sign up to the newsletter at www.beastquest.co.uk
to receive exclusive extra content and the opportunity to enter special members-only competitions.
We'll send you up-to-date info on all the Beast
Quest books, including the next exciting series
which features six brand-new Beasts!

All books priced at £4.99,
special bumper editions
priced at £5.99.

Orchard Books are available from all good bookshops, or can
be ordered from our website: www.orchardbooks.co.uk,
or telephone 01235 827702, or fax 01235 8227703.

Series 10: MASTER OF THE BEASTS
COLLECT THEM ALL!

An old enemy has come back to haunt Tom –
and unleash six awesome new Beasts!

NOCTILA
THE DEATH OWL

978 1 40831 518 7

SHAMANI
THE RAGING FLAME

978 1 40831 519 4

LUSTOR
THE ACID DART

978 1 40831 520 0

VOLTREX
THE TWO-HEADED OCTOPUS

978 1 40831 521 7

TECTON
THE ARMOURED GIANT

978 1 40831 522 4

DOOMSKULL
THE KING OF FEAR

978 1 40831 523 1